# GIRLZ

# Mummy Mania

## Holly Smith Dinbergs

illustrated by
## Monika Maddock

First published in 2006 by
MACMILLAN EDUCATION AUSTRALIA PTY LTD
627 Chapel Street, South Yarra, Australia 3141

This edition first published in the United States of America
in 2006 by MONDO Publishing.

For information contact:
MONDO Publishing
980 Avenue of the Americas
New York, NY 10018

Visit our web site at http://www.mondopub.com

06 07 08 09 10   9 8 7 6 5 4 3 2 1

ISBN 1-59336-935-2  (PB)

Series created by Felice Arena and Phil Kettle
Project Management by Limelight Press Pty Ltd
Cover and text design by Lore Foye
Illustrations by Monika Maddock

Printed in Hong Kong

# GIRLZ ROCK!

# Contents

*Jules*     *Rosa*

# CHAPTER 1

# Fan Plan

Jules and Rosa are sitting in the back seat of Jules's grandma's car on a sunny Saturday morning. Jules's grandma and her friend Ruby are taking the girls to the local museum.

**Rosa** "Did you see Video View this morning? Jemma Dazzle was on."

**Jules** "Yeah, I just saw the end of it. She's so cool."

**Rosa** "Jemma's in town for tonight's benefit concert at the showground."

**Jules** "I know. I'd love to see her but the show's sold out."

**Rosa** "It's on TV tonight though, so we can watch it at home."

**Jules** "I wonder where she stays when she's in town."

**Rosa**  "Hmm…it might be near here. Wouldn't it be cool if we saw her?"

The car passes a sign for the Egyptian exhibition at the museum.

**Rosa**  "What's this exhibition we're going to?"

**Jules** "I told Grandma we're studying Egypt. She thinks we should see some mummies and learn about all that stuff."

**Rosa** "Cool."

**Jules** "Ahhh, mummies are creepy."

Jules's grandma parks the car, and they all walk to the museum entrance. Rosa watches the people going inside.

**Rosa** "Jules, Jules, you'll never guess who I just saw."

**Jules** "Who?"

**Rosa** "Jemma Dazzle!"

**Jules** "No way!"

**Rosa** "Yeah, I'm sure it was her. No one else dresses like she does."

**Jules** "Jemma Dazzle here? I can't believe it!"

**Rosa** "C'mon, let's try to find her.
She's gotta be here somewhere."
**Jules** "This is a pretty big place. She
could be anywhere."

Just then, Jules's grandma walks
over with the tickets. She takes the
girls inside the museum.

# CHAPTER 2

# You Call That Art?

Jules's grandma suggests that they all meet in an hour at the museum cafe. Before leaving, she reminds the girls not to make any noise and not to run around.

**Jules** "Okay, Grandma."
**Rosa** "Quick, Jules, I think Jemma just walked by."

**Jules** "Where'd she go?"

**Rosa** "Uh...I'm not positive it was her. But she had bright green hair and lots of black around her eyes, you know, just like Jemma."

**Jules** "Cool, let's find her. Maybe we can get her autograph."

The girls enter a room with a sign on the door that says "Modern Art."

**Rosa** "Wow! Look at that!"

She points to an enormous painting hanging on a white wall.

**Jules** "It looks like something I painted when I was six."

**Rosa** "I think it looks like somebody spilled their drink on the canvas."

**Jules** (laughing) "Yeah, chocolate milkshake and vanilla cola."

**Rosa** "Mixed with orange juice."

The girls laugh so loud that a museum guide tells them to "shush."

**Jules** (whispering) "We're supposed to be quiet."

The girls pretend to study the painting, trying not to laugh. The museum guide tells the group in the room that it's worth $500,000.

**Rosa** "$500,000? For that?"

**Jules** "I know how we could make lots of money. Spill drinks on some paper and sell it!"

The girls burst out laughing again.

Just then, a woman with bright green hair and lots of black around her eyes walks past the door. Rosa tugs on Jules's arm.

**Rosa** "I just saw Jemma go that way."

The girls head off, on the trail of Jemma Dazzle.

# CHAPTER 3

# Paris at Night

At the end of the hallway, Jules finds a room with a sign on the door saying "Paris at Night."

**Jules** "Maybe Jemma went in here. Let's take a look."

The girls enter the room, which is very dark.

**Rosa** "They sure need to change the light bulbs in here."

The girls move aside as the tour group comes into the room. The guide explains that this room is dark because the pictures must be protected from bright light.

**Jules** (pointing) "Check out this painting."

**Rosa** "I dressed like that once for Halloween."

**Jules** "Look how the dancer's standing."

**Rosa** "Her legs are so close together, it's amazing she doesn't fall over."

**Jules** "Especially with her arm above her head like that. She looks kind of like the Statue of Liberty."

**Rosa** "Let me try that pose."

Rosa tries to get into the same
position as the girl in the painting.

**Rosa** "There. I look just like her."
**Jules** "I don't think so. Your arms
and legs aren't straight."

**Rosa** "They're straight enough."

**Jules** "Here, let me help."

Jules adjusts Rosa's legs and arms. As Rosa tries to straighten her legs and keep her arms in the right position, she loses her balance.

**Rosa** "Heeelp!"

Rosa falls over. The girls laugh as Jules helps Rosa up.

**Jules** "Uh-oh, there's that guide. Let's get outta here."

The girls continue down the hall to the last room, where the sign on the door says "Ancient Egypt."

**Jules** "This must be where the mummies are."

**Rosa** "I've never seen a real mummy."

**Jules** "Maybe Jemma's in there. It'd be so cool if we could actually talk to her. No one at school would believe it."

Jules follows Rosa into the room.

# CHAPTER 4

# Come to Mummy

The room is full of people but Jemma Dazzle is nowhere to be seen.

**Rosa** "Too bad, no Jemma. But look Jules, these wall paintings are just like the ones in our history book."

**Jules** "Weird. The men wore little white skirts."

**Rosa** "And they all have black around their eyes. Like Jemma."

**Jules**  "Didn't they walk funny?"
**Rosa**  "Yeah. Like this."

Rosa begins to walk with one arm bent in front, palm down, and one arm behind, palm up. Rosa leads them to a glass case, where the girls stop and stare.

**Rosa**  "Wow! A real live mummy."
**Jules**  "You mean a real *dead* mummy."

**Rosa** "Do you know how they make mummies? After you die, they pull your brain out your nose and wrap you in a bunch of rags."

**Jules** "Ahh, that's gross. This mummy's all tattered and dirty. Mummies look better in the movies. This one gives me the creeps."

Rosa walks slowly to the other side of the glass case.

**Rosa** "I think he's watching me."

**Jules** "Who? The mummy? News flash—this guy's dead."

**Rosa** "Are you sure? Mummies come back to life all the time."

**Jules** "No, they don't."

**Rosa** "I just walked away from him and his eyes followed me. I swear."

**Jules** "His eyes are all covered up. Stop it, Rosa, you're scaring me."

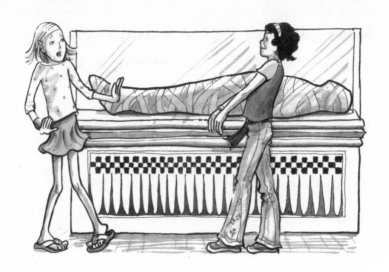

**Rosa** "How do you know he can't see? You don't know *what's* going on under those big bandages."

Jules edges toward the door. Rosa shuffles up to Jules with her arms out, doing her mummy walk.

**Rosa** (moaning) "I'm a muuuummy. I'm aliiive."

**Jules** "Stop it, Rosa. You're creeping me out!"

**Rosa** (moaning) "I'm a muuuummy.
I came baaaack to liiiife to get
youuuu."

Jules steps backward into the
hallway and crashes into a woman
with bright green hair and lots of black
around her eyes. Jules is so startled,
she screams.

**Jules**  "Aaaghh! Aaaaghhh! Sorry...
I...I...hey, you're not..."

By the time Jules calms down, the
woman with green hair is gone.

**Rosa**  "You okay, Jules? So did you
see her? It wasn't Jemma after all."

**Jules** "Nah, guess not, but it sure looked like her."

The girls see Jules's grandma and Ruby walking toward them, and they don't look happy.

**Rosa** "I have a feeling our museum visit is about to end."

# CHAPTER 5

# An Early Exit

Jules's grandma decides it's time to leave the museum—before lunch! The girls are really disappointed.

**Rosa**  "C'mon, Jules. I'm sorry for scaring you. I didn't mean to get you into trouble with your grandma."

With her eyes on the floor, Jules says nothing.

**Rosa** "I was just joking around. Mummies really are dead, y'know."

The girls follow Jules's grandma and Ruby along the corridor. Jules continues to ignore Rosa.

**Rosa** "I know we're leaving early 'cause we made too much noise, but you have to admit it was fun playing Jemma Dazzle detectives."

Jules still says nothing. Rosa doesn't know what to say, so she shuffles along behind Jules.

**Rosa** (softly) "I'm a siiiilly muuuummy without a brrraiin. Someone sucked it out through my noooose. I'm sooorry I scaaared yooou."

Jules smiles, then bursts out laughing. The girls shuffle like mummies down the hall.

**Jules** "Tiiime to gooo!"

**Rosa** "Hey, Jules, if it had really been Jemma Dazzle, what would you have done?"

**Jules** "Told her to watch out for the live mummy in the room!"

**Rosa** "I can't wait to see her on TV tonight."

**Jules** "Me too. It'll be better than almost seeing her here!"

The girls walk like Egyptians all the way back to the car.

GIRLZROCK!
# Mummy Lingo

Jules                                          Rosa

**archaeologist** A scientist who studies groups of people who lived in the past by looking at bones and other old stuff.

**embalming** A process used to stop a dead body from decaying and getting really gross.

**linen** What the ancient Egyptians used to wrap a mummy's body.

**mummy** The body of a person (or an animal) that has been embalmed after death.

**tattered** torn and ragged

**tomb** A room or building where a dead person is laid to rest.

33

# GIRLZ ROCK!
# Mummy Musts

☆ Learn to walk like an Egyptian: one arm in front, bent at the elbow and wrist, with your palm down; the other arm behind, palm up.

☆ If you're talking to a mummy, don't ask "Where's Daddy?" They've heard that joke a thousand times.

☆ Use a criss-cross pattern if you ever need to wrap a mummy with linen bandages.

☆ Mummies shouldn't hang around in the laundry room or they might get thrown into the washing machine with the other dirty linen.

☆ Watch scary mummy movies with your friends. A couple of good ones are *The Mummy* and *The Mummy Returns*.

☆ Mummies shouldn't drive convertibles because their linen bandages will flap in the wind and become loose—and then they might catch a cold!

☆ If you want to scare your friends on Halloween, dress up as a mummy and pretend you are coming after them.

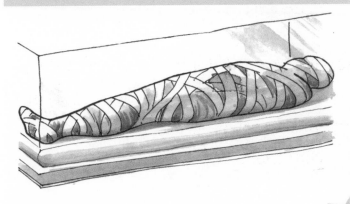

# GiRLZ ROCK!
# Mummy Instant Info

👁 Ancient Egyptians were master
mummy makers, but mummies
have been found all over the world,
including in China, South America, and
Greenland.

👁 To make a mummy, the dead body
has to be dried out using either the
sun, fire, smoke, or chemicals. The
Egyptians used a chemical called
natron to dry out dead bodies.

👁 In ancient Egypt, the embalming
process took about 70 days. It wasn't
easy making a mummy!

👁 Some mummies are so well
preserved that it's possible to see
what the person actually looked like
when he or she was alive.

When rich ancient Egyptians died, professional mourners were often hired for the funerals. These people would pretend they were sad by crying and throwing dirt on their hair.

Pharaohs (ancient Egyptian kings) and other rich Egyptians were buried with lots of valuable stuff like gold and jewels. Their tombs were often located in pyramids.

King Tutankhamen was a teenaged pharaoh who died in 1346 B.C. His tomb, which was discovered in 1922, contained a solid gold coffin and throne, jewelry, and other priceless objects.

# GIRLZ ROCK!
# Think Tank

1 What is the name of the singer who Rosa thinks she sees at the museum?

2 What is Rosa trying to imitate when she falls over?

3 What does Rosa do to make Jules mad?

4 What do you call a mummy's final resting place?

5 What kind of cloth are mummies wrapped in?

6 Do you think it was a good idea for Jules's grandma to let the girls walk around the museum on their own? Why or why not?

7 If you were Jules, would you have gotten mad at Rosa over what she did? Why or why not?

8 Have you ever seen a real mummy at a museum? What did you think of it?

# Answers

# How did you score?

- If you got most of the answers correct, think about studying archaeology. One day you could go to Egypt and look for real mummies!

- If you got more than half of the answers correct, write a play about mummies and perform it for your parents.

- If you got less than half of the answers correct, practice walking like an Egyptian instead.

*Hey, Girls!*

*I love to read and hope you do, too. The first book I really loved was a book called "Mary Poppins." It was full of magic (way before Harry Potter) and it got me hooked on reading. I went to the library every Saturday and left with a pile of books so heavy I could hardly carry them!*

*Here are some ideas about how you can make "Mummy Mania" even more fun. At school, you and your friends can be actors and put on this story as a play. To bring the story to life, use some props such as a big poster with bright colors spilled on it for modern art, or a picture of a ballerina. Maybe you can wrap someone up in toilet paper to play the mummy lying on a table.*

Who will be Jules? Who will be Rosa? Who will be the narrator? (That's the person who reads the parts between Jules or Rosa saying something.) Once you've decided on these details, you're ready to act out the story in front of the class. I bet everyone will clap when you are finished. Hey, a talent scout from a television station might just be watching!

See if someone at home will read this story out loud with you. Reading at home is important and a lot of fun as well.

You know what my dad used to tell me? Readers are leaders!

And remember, Girlz Rock!

Holly talked to Shey, another *Girlz Rock!* author.

**Shey** "Did you ever see a mummy at the museum when you were a kid?"

**Holly** "Yeah, lots of times."

**Shey** "Really? Were you scared?"

**Holly** "Not at all."

**Shey** "How come?"

**Holly** "It made me feel good inside."

**Shey** "If I saw a mummy, I think I'd be really scared."

**Holly** "No, you wouldn't. Not if it was *my* mummy. She's great!"

# GIRLZROCK!

# What a Laugh!

**Q** What's a mummy's favorite music?

**A** Wrap music.